GET READY...GET SET...READ!

WHAT A TRIP!

by
Foster & Erickson

Illustrations by
Kerri Gifford

BARRON'S

Bub and Chub
are in the sand.

Both of them have
a ship in hand.

Bub says, "I will take my ship on a very long trip."

Up, up, up
jets the space ship.

It whips around space.
It is so fast.

Then it rips and it dips
and it lands at last.

I open the ship.
I must get help.

But all I see is a
land of sand.

I zip here and there
and I look all around.

I want a drink, but there is
no drink to be found.

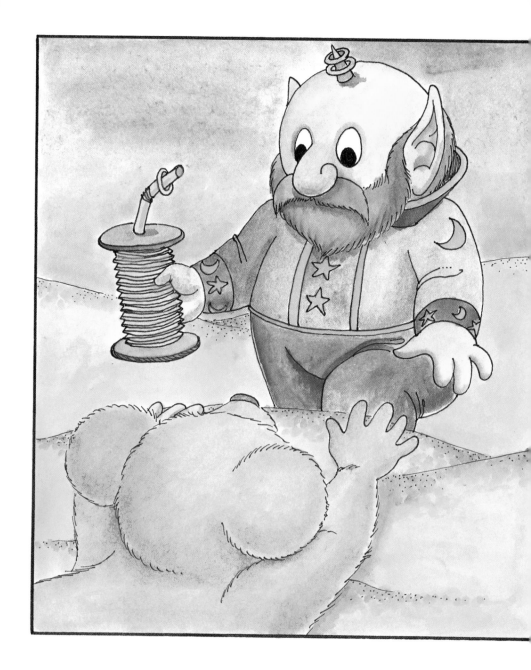

Then a small spaceman
comes to help me, I think.

"Glub, glub," he says.
And he hands me a drink.

Then he makes my
space ship look brand-new.

"Glub, glub," he says.
I say, "Thank you."

Then I land on the sand
where my trip began.

"What a trip!" says Chub.

Now Chub says, "I will take a trip on my fast ship."

Away whips my ship,
away from the sand.
Now I cannot see the land.

Skip and I are on the ship.

"Skip, you scrub
and I look," says the cub.

But then, what a hubbub!
A wind whips and jogs my ship.

The ship flips and dips
and then it tips. Slog-slog.

I trip and slip
out of the ship.

I look around, but there
is no help to be found.
"Glub, glub."

Then up comes Skip
in a sub.

He says, "Let me
help you, Chub"

Then we land on the sand
where my trip began.

"What a trip!" says Bub.

"Let's do it again,"
says Chub.

DEAR PARENTS AND EDUCATORS:

Welcome to **Get Ready...Get Set...Read!**

We've created these books to introduce children to the magic of reading.

Each story in the series is built around one or two word families. For example, *A Mop for Pop* uses the OP word family. Letters and letter blends are added to OP to form words such as TOP, LOP, and STOP.

This **Bring-It-All-Together** book serves as a reading review. When your children have finished *Jake and the Snake, Jeepers Creepers, Two Fine Swine, What Rose Does Not Know,* and *Pink and Blue,* it is time to have them read this book. *Hide and Seek* uses the characters and words introduced in set 3 of **Get Ready . . . Get Set . . . Read!** (Each set in the series will be followed by two review books.)

Bring-It-All-Together books provide:
• much needed vocabulary repetition for developing fluency.
• longer stories for increasing reading attention spans.
• new stories with familiar characters for motivating young readers.

We have created these **Bring-It-All-Together** books to help develop confidence and competence in your young reader. We wish you much success in your reading adventures.

Kelli C. Foster, PhD   Gina Clegg Erickson, MA
Educational Psychologist   Reading Specialist

All inquiries should be addressed to:
Barron's Educational Series, Inc.
250 Wireless Boulevard
Hauppauge, NY 11788

International Standard Book Number 0-8120-1923-7
Library of Congress Catalog Card Number: 94-15219

PRINTED IN HONG KONG
19 18 17 16 15 14 13 12 11 10

Titles in the

Series

SET 1

Find Nat
The Sled Surprise
Sometimes I Wish
A Mop for Pop
The Bug Club
BRING-IT-ALL-TOGETHER BOOKS
What a Day for Flying!
Bat's Surprise

SET 2

The Tan Can
The Best Pets Yet
Pip and Kip
Frog Knows Best
Bub and Chub
BRING-IT-ALL-TOGETHER BOOKS
Where Is the Treasure?
What a Trip!

SET 3

Jake and the Snake
Jeepers Creepers
Two Fine Swine
What Rose Doesn't Know
Pink and Blue
BRING-IT-ALL-TOGETHER BOOKS
The Pancake Day
Hide and Seek

SET 4

Whiptail of Blackshale Trail
Colleen and the Bean
Dwight and the Trilobite
The Old Man at the Moat
By the Light of the Moon
BRING-IT-ALL-TOGETHER BOOKS
Night Light
The Crossing

SET 5

Tall and Small
Bounder's Sound
How to Catch a Butterfly
Ludlow Grows Up
Matthew's Brew
BRING-IT-ALL-TOGETHER BOOKS
Snow in July
Let's Play Ball